Villainous Stars

Ancel Mondia

Ukiyoto Publishing

All global publishing rights are held by

Ukiyoto Publishing

Published in 2023

Content Copyright © Ancel Mondia

ISBN 9789359202051

*All rights reserved.
No part of this publication may be reproduced,
transmitted, or stored in a retrieval system, in any form
by any means, electronic, mechanical, photocopying,
recording or otherwise, without the prior permission of
the publisher.*

The moral rights of the authors have been asserted.

*This is a work of fiction. Names, characters, businesses,
places, events, locales, and incidents are either the
products of the author's imagination or used in a fictitious
manner. Any resemblance to actual persons, living or
dead, or actual events is purely coincidental.*

*This book is sold subject to the condition that it shall not by
way of trade or otherwise, be lent, resold, hired out or
otherwise circulated, without the publisher's prior
consent, in any form of binding or cover other than that in
which it is published.*

www.ukiyoto.com

Contents

Aranea	1
Cancer	7
Corvus	13
Lepus	19
Noctua	25
Pavo	31
About the Author	36

Aranea

In a fast-paced city where multiple passersby were in their work and school uniforms, a lady in rural clothing was mindlessly walking with a gloomy face. Her teary eyes slowly looked around and suddenly got fixed on the sight of a typical restaurant. She weakly lifted her feet to silently enter through the glass door.

She went directly to the vacant bar counter and a female bartender gladly approached her. The bartender instantly noticed the gloomy face of the lady as the bartender hesitantly handed a filled wine glass to the lady. The female bartender silently studied the weak appearance of the lady when the lady suddenly noticed the obvious curiosity of the bartender.

"Why are you staring at me that way?" The lady asked with irritability in her voice.

The female bartender surprisingly stammered. "I'm sorry if you're bothered. I just wonder if you have a problem."

The lady abruptly sniffed and quivered. "It was decades ago when my mother died after giving birth to us. I have a twin brother, and we live together with our aging father. But I've never been happy being with them. I feel that Papa has been blaming me for Mama's death. Papa only loves Brother. Because they're both men. And I'm not."

The female bartender remained utterly silent as pity was strongly shown by her face.

The lady pensively continued. "But I don't hate Brother. I don't hate Papa. I just want to breathe. To somehow leave the house to be somewhere else. Where I can forget my loneliness even for a while."

The bartender gently held the shaky hand of the lady. "You can be here. You can work here if you want. Come back here tomorrow and we'll work together."

"Papa and Brother don't allow me to work. They think I can only do the household chores." The lady shamefully admitted.

"Prove them wrong. You can't be like that forever." The bartender loudly insisted.

All of a sudden, the glass door forcibly banged and a young man entered the typical restaurant. His mad facial expression matched his thundering shout as his searching eyes directly laid on the lady. "Aranea!"

The lady instantly startled when her teary eyes met the stern look of the young man. "Brother."

The young man suddenly clutched Aranea by her arm and dragged her with him to exit the typical restaurant. The female bartender was still in shock as she quietly watched the twins as they entered their shiny car and quickly left the busy street.

After the emotional scene made by the twins, the ordinariness of the day was experienced in the typical restaurant. The female bartender mindfully shrugged her shoulders as an obvious sign of forgetting the lady and her twin brother.

The next day naturally brightened the fast-paced city and the female bartender was happily working in the typical restaurant when she unexpectedly saw Aranea showing up before her. Aranea obviously looked tired and confused but shyly smiled at the bartender.

"Hello, my friend." Aranea calmly greeted the bartender.

The bartender confusingly replied. "Hello. How may I help you?"

Aranea hesitantly smiled. "Have you forgotten? You offered me to work here. I'm here to work."

"What?! What about your father and brother?" The bartender loudly queried.

Aranea suddenly stammered. "I left the house without telling them. But they can't do anything if I've already started working here. They'll be too shy to stop me."

All of a sudden, they alarmingly heard deafening squealing tires followed by a blasting vehicle bump. Aranea and the female bartender quickly went outside the typical restaurant and shockingly saw the tragic accident. Before them was an unknown truck that was extremely damaged and a shattered car whose driver and passenger were bloody and motionless.

Aranea strongly trembled in powerful fear as she feebly walked towards her brother's car. She instantly saw the dead faces of her twin brother and old father. Aranea loudly screamed in deep pain and strong guilt.

"This is my fault! I killed Papa and Brother!"

The bartender pitifully embraced Aranea and they heavily cried together. Aranea strangely stared at the bartender as the bartender sympathetically tried to comfort her.

Ordinary days simply passed by as Aranea and the female bartender worked together in the typical restaurant. Almost every instance that the bartender was busy at the bar counter, Aranea looked at the bartender with intense hate in her eyes.

One dark evening, Aranea was silently observing the female bartender when Aranea surprisingly saw a nondescript guy sweetly handing the happy bartender a flower bouquet. Aranea shook her head in strong contempt and subtly hid a sinister smile.

Aranea gladly joined the happy couple. "Friend, won't you introduce me to your lover?"

The innocent bartender widely smiled. "Aranea, this is my lover. Love, this is Aranea."

The bartender's lover anticipatedly acted amiable towards Aranea.

Aranea excitedly spoke. "You two should take a seat. I'll prepare a wine. Let's have a drink."

The young lovers happily sat together as Aranea quickly turned her back to gracefully pour the red wine in three clear wine glasses. She carefully pulled out a dark small bottle and silently poured and mixed its liquid with the wine.

Aranea calmly handed the nondescript guy and the female bartender a filled wine glass. The bartender's lover instantly drank the wine and Aranea's face suddenly lit in triumph. The nondescript guy had extreme difficulty in breathing and the bartender crazily panicked. In a short while, the bartender's lover completely turned lifeless.

The female bartender cried heavily. "What have you done, Aranea?! Why?!"

Aranea proudly replied. "He deserves that. It's your fault, friend."

"What?! I don't understand." The bartender innocently asked.

"It's my revenge for Papa and Brother. Because you offered me to work here, they tried to stop me. So they died. Because of you, I lost my family. It's your fault. You can't be happy while I'm miserable. You deserve to feel the pain of losing someone you love as you caused me." Aranea emotionally spoke.

The bartender painfully insisted. "Nobody wanted it, Aranea. It was an accident."

Aranea nonchalantly lifted her filled wine glass. "I have finally avenged your death. Papa. Brother. I have no more reason to live." Aranea suddenly drank the poisonous wine and instantly dropped dead.

Aranea's human flesh horribly tore and formed into countless spiders that quickly crawled all over the typical restaurant and towards the busy street. Some spiders that were fatally pressed by the running vehicles' tires lifted towards the night sky and formed into twinkling stars.

The female bartender confusingly exited the typical restaurant to curiously look at the night sky with the twinkling stars that vaguely formed into a spider constellation that painfully reminded her of a lady named Aranea.

Cancer

A luxurious car smoothly arrived in an expensive-looking beach resort which was meticulously adorned with vibrant flowers and silk fabrics. At the center was a spacious pavilion orderly occupied by crafted tables and chairs with sumptuous foods and drinks. The male guests were in dress pants and collared shirts, while the female guests were in summer sundresses and dressy sandals.

From the luxurious car ungracefully came out the male driver and his two female passengers that obviously looked like a well-off family. The irritable man swiftly left his nagging wife, as his shy daughter quietly walked behind him.

"Don't get drunk! Don't you dare put me to shame here!" The wife loudly shouted.

"She's too noisy. Doesn't she know that she's the shameful one?" The man angrily whispered.

The irritable man suddenly noticed his shy daughter behind him. "Cancer, we're late already. Walk fast."

The shy daughter clearly called by her name Cancer simply nodded her head.

Her nagging mother, who was still sitting inside their luxurious car, loudly shouted again. "Cancer! Come back here! Brush your hair first!"

"Ignore her. She's just being overly conscious about our looks." The father quickly whispered to his daughter.

Cancer quietly nodded her head again.

Her mother irritably came out of their luxurious car and obviously rushed towards her daughter, when they were surprisingly welcomed by a well-dressed couple.

"Welcome to our wedding anniversary!" The aged couple cheerfully greeted them.

The well-off family awkwardly replied. "Happy wedding anniversary!"

The father who instantly pretended to be calm quickly apologized. "We're sorry if we're late."

The cheerful man, with his female partner, gracefully responded. "It's okay. Good thing is you've arrived."

His female partner proudly spoke. "We're really happy that you're here to celebrate our wedding anniversary with us. You know what, I am so lucky with my husband. I have an incredibly wonderful married life because of him. And I know for sure that he feels the same way too."

The cheerful couple heartily laughed together, and Cancer's mother suddenly interrupted them. "We also have a great married life, especially that we are blessed with a daughter."

The cheerful man immediately looked at Cancer and curiously asked. "Is she your daughter?"

Cancer's father quickly replied. "Yes. Her name is Cancer."

The cheerful man suddenly became extremely excited. "Great! We have a son."

"Are you talking about me?" A young man surprisingly appeared before them.

Cancer slowly lifted her head and shyly met the sparkling eyes of the young man who cheerfully greeted her. "Hello, Cancer. It's my pleasure to meet you."

Cancer gracefully answered. "It's my pleasure to meet you too."

After their first conversation, Cancer and the young man subtly exchanged flirtatious stares to each other as the grand celebration went on. The young man quietly approached Cancer as Cancer stood still waiting for him.

The young man clearly whispered to her. "Let's meet here tomorrow morning."

Cancer submissively nodded her head.

When the grand celebration was obviously concluded, Cancer mysteriously stared at the young man before she slowly went inside her family's luxurious car that eventually left the expensive-looking beach resort.

The next day, the vibrant flowers and silk fabrics were all removed, and the pavilion was completely cleaned and left vacant. The sun was slowly setting down when the young man was impatiently walking back and forth. All of a sudden, he saw Cancer shyly approaching him.

"Cancer, why are you late?" The young man loudly asked.

"I'm sorry. I was doubting if I should come here." Cancer uncomfortably apologized.

The young man instantly became calm and slowly caressed Cancer's face. "It's okay, Cancer."

His head quickly moved close to Cancer but Cancer instantly avoided him.

Cancer confusingly asked. "What are you doing?"

The young man annoyingly smiled. "I'm about to kiss you. I know you want it."

Cancer abruptly shook her head with disbelief all over her face.

The young man teasingly continued. "Don't play hard to get, Cancer."

Cancer suddenly yelled at him. "How rude you are! I shouldn't have come here."

The young man insultingly laughed. "Cancer, don't forget that you're a lady. You should act shy and submissive."

Cancer frighteningly spoke. "I thought you're a good man because your parents are happily married. I thought you're good because your father seems good."

"They look happily married because Mother is submissive and Father is aggressive. But you really don't know what's going on in our house. Don't be naive, Cancer. I know your family is dysfunctional. If you want a good man, be a good lady."

"I was wrong for coming here." Cancer boldly spoke and turned her back.

The young man swiftly held Cancer and desperately tried to kiss her, but Cancer strongly resisted him. They intensely fought until the warm sun thoroughly disappeared in the horizon.

Cancer gradually grew weak, and the young man was about to triumphantly act on his obnoxious motive, when Cancer shockingly bit his sweaty neck.

The young man suddenly released her due to the painful bite. He was about to boldly attack her when Cancer crazily scratched his body with her sharp nails and repeatedly bit his face with her sharp teeth.

The young man gradually fell on the white sand stained by his fresh blood. When he eventually became motionless, Cancer completely stopped her horrible attack.

For the first time, masculine pride was in her feminine demeanor. Cancer intentionally stared at the waving sea and swiftly dashed towards it until she completely submerged in the waters.

After a short while, multiple crabs were scattered by the waving sea on the sandy seashore. Some crabs that remained floating in the waters lighted up and wondrously went up to the night sky and mysteriously formed into the crab constellation.

The young man, motionlessly lying on the sand, weakly opened his dull eyes and shockingly witnessed the frightening brightness of the constellation he silently called Cancer.

Corvus

The stormy afternoon dimmed the center of a dense woodland where a normal school, which was typically known for training teachers, was silently situated. A female trainee, under her plain umbrella, was casually walking around the rain-soaked campus. All of a sudden, she was harshly grabbed by her weak shoulder. Her long black hair violently swayed as she confusingly turned her head to see the attacker.

Her shocked eyes met the mad and wet countenance of another female trainee. The attacker quickly slapped her pale face and forcefully pushed her slender body. She involuntarily stepped backward due to the unanticipated offense.

The offended female trainee painfully stared at her mad attacker. She bizarrely remained silent as her plain umbrella shadowed her pale face. The mad attacker suddenly widened her piercing eyes as she spoke with a shrill voice.

"What, Corvus?! Say something!"

The offended female trainee strangely stayed tight-lipped.

"Doesn't it hurt, Corvus?" The attacker insultingly asked.

Corvus slowly spoke with a deep voice. "Why are you doing this?"

The attacker abruptly raised her voice in disbelief. "You don't know?! You're extremely naive. I thought we were friends. You were supposed to help me in our training. But you didn't. See, I failed. While you topped the exams!"

Corvus slightly shook her head in defense. "We don't need to cheat. And you can't depend on me all the time. It's not my fault if you failed. That's your own doing."

The attacker deafeningly yelled at Corvus. "You're selfish! You're a fake friend! There's nothing of you that's real. You only think of favor to be all yours."

Corvus suddenly raised her voice. "You can't tell me what I am! You can't dictate to me what I'm supposed to do! I have my own belief about what is right and wrong. And I'll follow what I know!"

"Really? Corvus, you're a mama's girl. You don't think on your own. Have you forgotten? Your mama is one of the trainers here. What do you think she will do if she finds out about your nasty behavior? She will scold you like a spoiled brat." The attacker assuredly threatened Corvus.

Corvus deepened her voice. "Don't use my mother against me. She trained me to be nice. But she also trained me to stand for myself."

The attacker sinisterly smiled. "But you can't stand against her."

Suddenly, the attacker violently pulled Corvus' long black hair, obviously trying to make her weakly kneel on the wet ground. But Corvus strongly counterattacked by repeatedly beating her attacker with the use of her plain umbrella.

The two female trainees intensely fought as they thoroughly got drenched by the heavy rain. All of a sudden, a male trainer caught them on the campus. He alarmingly rushed towards them and gradually stood between the female trainees.

"Stop! You two, stop!" The male trainer mightily shouted.

The two female trainees simultaneously stood still, but they remained madly staring at each other.

The male trainer loudly scolded them. "You shouldn't fight here! You are trainees! Don't you know?! You can destroy our school's reputation!"

The female attacker suddenly talked back. "It's you, sir, who can destroy this school's reputation! You have favoritism! Why Corvus?! Because she's your type?!"

"What?! What are you saying?!" The male trainer's voice angrily raised.

All of a sudden, they were interrupted by a woman's deep voice. "What's happening?"

The two female trainees and the male trainer simultaneously turned their heads to shockingly see a woman trainer under her plain umbrella proudly standing before them.

"Mother?" Corvus uttered in trembling fright.

"You, trainees. Follow me. And you, trainer. Stay here." Corvus' mother clearly ordered.

The male trainer silently nodded, while Corvus and her attacker simply followed the woman trainer. The three females slowly entered a vacant room, and the woman trainer proudly sat before a wooden table.

"Shut the door, and sit." The woman trainer coldly ordered.

The two female trainees simply obeyed, and silently faced each other.

The woman trainer nonchalantly spoke. "Corvus, apologize to her."

Corvus instantly got shocked and confusingly talked to her mother. "Why, Mother?"

"Don't dare to disobey me, Corvus." The woman trainer suddenly deepened her voice.

"No!" Corvus emotionally replied.

The female attacker sinisterly smiled.

Corvus' mother angrily raised her voice. "I'm your mother! Obey me!"

"You trained me to be nice. But not to the extent that I can't stand for myself. I'd believed and obeyed you. But not this time. You side with her without even asking what really happened!" Corvus spoke in pain and disbelief.

"This is for your betterment. This is for the peace of our school." Corvus' mother calmly said.

"No! This is for your reputation." Corvus replied in anger.

The shocked woman trainer suddenly looked at the confused female attacker. "You, trainee. Go now. Leave us."

The female attacker quickly stood up and left Corvus with her mother.

Corvus' mother emotionally scolded Corvus. "Why did you shame me, Corvus?! Be nice! I keep telling you that! Be nice!"

Corvus madly stared at her trembling mother. "I can stand for myself even if it means standing against you."

Corvus proudly turned her back and exited the room. The woman trainer painfully held her chest and instantly fell on the floor. Corvus casually walked around the rain-soaked campus, and the male trainer surprisingly saw her. The male trainer curiously called her but Corvus mindlessly ignored him.

All of a sudden, Corvus swiftly ran towards the opened metal gate of the normal school. She crazily proceeded at the dense woodland as the stormy afternoon instantly became wilder and darker. Under the violently swaying trees, she unstoppably moved.

In the blink of an eye, a huge branch broke and fell on Corvus. The storm relentlessly continued in the evening. But when the weather gradually calmed and the moon mysteriously shone, Corvus' dead body slowly blackened and turned into feathers. The male trainer standing from a distance suddenly saw soaring crows from the woody area where Corvus fell. Multiple crows freely flew at the dense woodland, and some of them directly soared towards the night sky. They swiftly burned, lighted up, and formed into the crow constellation, the male trainer called Corvus.

Lepus

A vast orchard gradually turned abundant with vibrant and ripe fruits, and multiple workers diligently and joyfully harvested the nutritious crops. The huge wooden baskets were quickly filled with different fruits and carefully carried to the bulky trucks.

A male worker repeatedly looked over his broad shoulder as his stern eyes obviously lingered on a female worker. He silently observed the female worker who was mentally occupied by the physical work she was doing. He looked straight at her basket several times as she speedily put the fruits inside.

When her basket was obviously filled, she was instantly handed another basket to fill. The male worker weakly turned his back and slowly stared at his basket which was half full. His trembling hand was about to reach a ripe fruit when he suddenly stopped and irritably sighed. He intentionally stared at the female worker and casually approached her.

"Lepus, why do you work too fast?" He annoyingly asked.

The female worker effortlessly continued the physical work while calmly answering him.

"Because I need to. I need coins for my sister's medicine."

The male worker loudly emphasized. "But you work too much!"

Lepus suddenly paused and confusingly looked at the male worker.

"What's wrong with how I work?" She innocently asked.

"You have filled several baskets already. I haven't filled one yet." He irritably said.

"What's wrong with that?" Lepus eagerly queried.

"Lepus, it's not good for you to do more than a male does." The male worker clearly stated.

Lepus strongly shook her head and annoyingly replied. "I'm not competing against you. I'm only doing my job."

All of a sudden, the heated conversation between the two workers was interrupted by an old man's voice.

"What are you doing?"

Lepus and the male worker quickly turned their heads and saw an old man who obviously emitted an air of authority.

"I'm not paying you to gossip. Do the work now." The old man sternly ordered.

The two workers instantly nodded and worked again at different speeds. The old man proudly stood near them and attentively observed Lepus and the male worker.

The old man insultingly laughed. "How can a female outrun a male?"

The male worker suddenly paused and directly asked the old man. "What do you mean, sir?"

The old man angrily answered. "You work too slow! You're male but you're weak."

The loud insult from the old man suddenly caught the attention of the rest of the workers as they turned their heads to curiously look at the humiliated male worker.

The male worker obviously tried to remain calm as he quickly looked at Lepus who was pitifully staring at him.

"This is your fault!" The male worker sternly said to Lepus.

The old man insultingly laughed again and loudly spoke to all the workers in the orchard. "Tomorrow is your pay day! And for those who filled more baskets, there'll be extra coins!"

The workers simultaneously rejoiced around the proud old man who slowly turned his back to leave the orchard on that day. The next day expectedly came and the workers were obviously excited for their pay.

The old man proudly arrived and gladly talked to the smiling workers. "Don't be too excited too fast. You'll have your coins this afternoon."

The workers, including Lepus, diligently and joyfully continued to harvest vibrant and ripe fruits. The male worker expectedly observed Lepus again, and his envious eyes steadily turned fierce.

When the afternoon apparently arrived, the workers happily gathered in an area of the vast orchard. Lepus casually stood and turned her back to a filled huge wooden basket behind her. The male worker silently passed behind Lepus without her knowledge.

After a short while, the old man irritably approached the happy workers. He proudly stood in front of them, and the workers instantly paid attention.

"Admit now! Or all of you will not be paid!" The old man angrily shouted.

The workers confusingly reacted and looked at one another.

"Somebody stole a bag of coins! Who among you is the thief?!" The old man sternly asked.

The male worker sinisterly smiled, and suddenly turned his head with an innocent face. His eyes abruptly turned frightened when he directly stared at the basket behind Lepus.

"Lepus, what's that behind you?" The male worker loudly asked Lepus.

Lepus surprisingly looked at the male worker and confusingly looked over her shoulder. Her questioning eyes quickly bulged in fright. The old man angrily approached Lepus.

"What's that?" The old man asked with suspicion in his voice.

The old man quickly looked at the filled huge wooden basket behind Lepus and shockingly saw a bag of coins. He madly stared at Lepus who was shaking her head in denial.

"You're the thief. You're the thief!" The old man emotionally accused her.

"I don't know how it got there." Lepus frighteningly said.

"You won't get paid because of your stealing." The old man said madly.

"I didn't steal that. I don't steal. I am not a thief!" Lepus painfully defended herself.

"I'll punish you for stealing my bag of coins!" The old man spoke threateningly.

The old man was about to hold the bag of coins when Lepus quickly held it first. Lepus instantly distanced from the shocked old man. Lepus' face turned extremely bold as she madly shouted.

"You'll punish me for the stealing that I didn't do?! I'd never stolen coins though I badly needed them for my sister! I've worked hard! I've worked hard for these coins! But if you accuse me of stealing, I'd rather steal these coins!"

Lepus suddenly ran away from the rest of the shocked workers, and the deceitful male worker quickly ran after her while shouting at Lepus to return the bag of coins to the old man. But Lepus was too fast for the male worker to capture. When the dusk unnoticeably arrived, Lepus shockingly reached an unforeseen cliff, but instead of stopping with second thought, she crazily jumped.

In the invisible air, the gold coins wildly flew and Lepus eerily transformed into multiple hares which instantly scattered everywhere. Some of the hares quickly soared to the dark sky as their bodies brightly illuminated and formed into the hare constellation. The exhausted male worker weakly stood near the cliff and madly shouted the name Lepus.

Noctua

Amid the vast grassland stood a secondary school whose instructors and learners were widely known for intelligence and excellence. The instructors steadily promoted quality education and discipline, while the learners constantly modeled good performance and character.

The secondary school obviously signified the shared dream of academic youth and teaching professionals because of its good reputation and outstanding brand. With the same aim to eternalize their legacy, the instructors of the secondary school intensely competed to be loudly recognized as the best schoolteacher.

However, despite the relentless effort and tough commitment of the instructors, no one among them seemed to outwork and outshine a female instructor commonly called Miss Noctua. She was steadily deemed the epitome of sagacity and credibility based on her interactions with her colleagues and learners.

Noctua obviously savored every moment she confidently spoke in front of her interested and entertained class. However, among her smart and nice learners was a female learner that repeatedly showed boredom and irritability towards Noctua. But the best schoolteacher simply ignored her female learner's unpleasant attitude and professionally taught various lessons.

Noctua genuinely smiled and gently asked her attentive class. "Any questions, class?"

The young learners promptly answered in unison. "No, Miss Noctua."

Noctua gladly spoke. "Great! So tomorrow I'll be giving you an exam."

The young learners instantly reacted in different ways due to excitement, worry, and surprise.

The female learner suddenly interrupted the class. "Why don't you give it now?!"

Noctua and the rest of the class immediately gave their attention to the female learner.

The female learner proudly continued. "Nothing will change if you'll give the exam now or tomorrow, Miss Noctua. I'll still fail. Because you don't like me."

Noctua slowly shook her head and calmly spoke. "Please don't say that."

"Oh, come on! You only like smart learners because they can quickly understand you. But you know what? I can't understand you. You're too complicated and difficult." The female learner irritably said.

"So you hate me? Nothing is simple and easy all the time. Because it's a way for us to study and learn." Noctua replied with composure.

The female learner abruptly stood up and annoyingly said. "Enough of wise words. I'm sick of hearing them." And instantly walked out from the silenced class.

Noctua remained standing in apparent shock, but she slowly looked at the rest of her young learners with hope and delight in her eyes. She quietly sighed and calmly spoke. "Class dismissed."

With hesitation and care in their facial expressions, the young learners slowly left Noctua alone.

When the best schoolteacher was in her solitude, she silently cried obviously due to the disrespect and hatred she directly received from her female learner. But she eventually wiped her hidden tears and confidently exited the vacant classroom.

With composure, Noctua walked down the hallway and felt the afternoon breeze. She quietly stood before a closed door, turned the doorknob, and opened her office. When she stepped in, her face suddenly turned shocked and angry.

Noctua saw scattered papers on the table and floor, as a young female learner in school uniform was violently opening the drawers.

"Who are you?!" Noctua madly spoke.

The learner shockingly turned her head and showed her face. Noctua's eyes suddenly bulged in disbelief and pain, as they clearly reflected the guilty face of the female learner.

"What are you doing?!" Noctua angrily asked.

The female learner was obviously confused, but she eventually looked straight at Noctua's pained and mad face.

"I'm looking for the answer key." The female learner proudly admitted.

"How dare you invade my space! How dare you cheat!" Noctua madly spoke.

"I'm desperate, Miss Noctua!" The female learner loudly said.

All of a sudden, Noctua strongly slapped her female learner. "Don't talk back to me!"

"Miss Noctua!" A shocked male voice instantly rang in Noctua's ears.

Noctua quickly turned her head, as the female learner suddenly burst into tears.

"Mister Principal?" Noctua uttered in shock.

"I came here with the intent to talk to the best schoolteacher. But what I saw deeply shocked me." The male school principal spoke in disbelief and confusion.

Noctua shamefully faced the school principal, as the female learner hurriedly left the chaotic office.

"Please let me explain, Mister Principal." Noctua painfully begged.

"There's no need to explain anything. I saw you. I caught you." The school principal said madly.

Noctua instantly burst into tears.

The school principal sternly spoke. "Miss Noctua, you're fired!"

Noctua cried louder as she weakly trembled and knelt before the school principal.

"I've given my all. I've given my best. For my profession. For this school. This is my life. Please forgive me if I fall short. I won't do it again. Please give me another chance." Noctua desperately begged.

The school principal quickly shook his head.

Noctua weakly stood up and slowly left the chaotic office. When she anticipatedly appeared in the hallway, the young learners simultaneously stared at her with judgment. Noctua silently exited the secondary school, as the school principal directly watched her in secret.

Noctua mindlessly wandered in the vast grassland as the darkness of the night gradually spread to the clear sky. She suddenly stood still in silence and forcefully screamed in deep pain. She sobbed heavily and repeatedly beat herself until she apparently felt exhausted.

She slowly embraced herself tight and blankly looked up to the night sky. A full moon shone brightly above her, and her whole body eerily glowed. She silently rested her both arms at her sides. After a short while, she gracefully lifted her arms as if she was about to freely fly. Feathers magically grew from her skin, and she swiftly flapped her arms. Her both feet suddenly lifted from the grassland, and her eerie figure instantly formed into multiple owls aimlessly flying in the air.

Some of the owls swiftly flew towards the night sky, strongly glowed and marked the darkness above with the owl constellation. The connected light of the mysterious group of stars clearly reflected in the school principal's terrified eyes, as his trembling mouth uttered the name Noctua.

Pavo

At a lofty and lush mountain where the warm sun shone blazingly, towering and shady trees boomingly fell one after another. Multiple loggers diligently acted on their typical duty with the use of their hand-held chainsaws and felling machines.

They carefully trimmed the limbs, meticulously sliced the logs, and energetically transported the timber. Both male and female loggers were apparently experienced and competent as they collectively demonstrated their logging skills.

In a soundless and composed manner, a woman in flamboyant clothing arrived at the work site. She subtly yet obviously acted as the well-off owner of the private broad forest. She modestly observed the multiple loggers when a male logger boldly showed romantic interest to her.

"What a great day, Madam Pavo! You're such a lovely sight to behold!" The male logger loudly greeted and praised her.

Pavo slightly showed irritation but instantly acted in politeness. "Thank you."

The woman in flamboyant clothing immediately ignored the flirty male logger, and casually walked around with searching eyes. Pavo slowly stopped before a female logger who quickly paused from cutting a tree from the moment their eyes directly met.

Pavo obviously turned sweet and gentle. "How's the work?"

The surprised female logger stammered. "It's doable, Madam Pavo."

Pavo mysteriously smiled. "Call me Pavo. No need to say Madam."

The confused female logger nodded. "Yes, Pavo."

"It's good to hear you say my name." Pavo seriously said.

The female logger apparently studied Pavo's radiant face, as Pavo simply stared at the female logger. The female logger suddenly shook her head in disbelief, and Pavo's expression turned curious.

"What's wrong?" Pavo tenderly asked.

The female logger obviously looked hesitant to answer.

"Say it." Pavo sweetly said.

"Do you like me?" The female logger embarrassingly asked.

Pavo suggestively smiled and assuredly nodded. "Yes."

The female logger's face initially showed disgust that she quickly concealed by a blank stare.

Pavo seemingly failed to notice her natural reaction, and continued to talk charmingly. "Since I first saw you, I fell hard for you."

The female logger replied in confusion. "But I am not a man. We're both women."

Pavo instantly turned irritated. "It's only our bodies. Our feelings are different."

"I don't understand. That's not normal. That's not acceptable." The female logger clearly spoke.

Pavo's face suddenly dimmed, as her aura apparently turned weak and pained, and her low voice cracked. "Are you rejecting me?"

The female logger looked utterly shocked. "What?! I'm a woman. And you're not a man."

Pavo instantly looked mad and forcefully repeated her question. "Are you rejecting me?!"

The female logger seemingly gained the courage to answer with certainty. "Yes! I'm rejecting you!"

Pavo thoughtlessly stood still as she utterly failed to notice the afternoon breeze.

The female logger quickly packed her things as she looked eager to leave the work site. She was about to turn her back when she boldly faced Pavo.

With anger in her voice and disgust in her face, the female logger spoke. "This is the last time you see me."

Pavo remained speechless, as the female logger hurriedly left the work site without even looking over her shoulder.

Without Pavo's knowledge, the male logger who boldly showed interest to her, silently witnessed the rejection that instantly followed her confession.

The evening gradually came, and the rest of the loggers normally left the work site. Pavo stayed alone at her privately owned forest.

Pavo secretly began to cry heavily and beat herself repeatedly. All of a sudden, the male logger showed up before her.

In shock and shame, Pavo asked. "Why are you here?!"

The male logger calmly answered. "I know what happened."

Pavo turned silent as if she certainly understood the male logger's implied reply.

The male logger slowly touched Pavo's hands and arms. "Let me comfort you."

Pavo abruptly looked confused. "What are you saying?"

The male logger suggestively smiled and clearly whispered. "Let me make you feel like a woman."

The male logger suddenly hugged Pavo tight.

Pavo quickly tried to free herself from the male logger's arms but she instantly failed.

The male logger harshly attempted to strip Pavo's flamboyant clothing, but Pavo suddenly turned wildly strong. They crazily fought as the male logger obviously desired to possess Pavo, and Pavo extremely wanted to save herself.

All of a sudden, Pavo's rough hands reached a sharp chainsaw and powerfully swayed its deadly teeth upon the male logger's neck. Fresh blood abruptly splashed in the air and terribly stained Pavo's face. The male logger instantly dropped dead and was beheaded.

Extreme fear and shock uncontrollably transpired in Pavo's entire being. Darkness thoroughly filled her human eyes, as guilt madly rushed through her core.

Pavo swiftly started to run under towering and shady trees as she deafeningly screamed in fathomless pain at the lofty and lush mountain.

Her human form rapidly grew flamboyant feathers, and when she unexpectedly stumbled, her human body utterly disappeared and eerily transformed into multiple peacocks.

The peacocks crazily scattered everywhere and some of them flew swiftly towards the night sky. Their feathers blazingly burned in the air, and unbelievably turned into stars that frighteningly formed into the peacock constellation.

The cut head of the male logger was facing the night sky where the peacock constellation mysteriously shone and clearly reflected by his opened still eyes, while his dead lips utterly failed to utter the flamboyant woman's name Pavo.

About the Author

Ancel Mondia

Ancel Mondia was awarded Fiction - Woman Writer of the Year by Ukiyoto Publishing in 2023.

www.ingramcontent.com/pod-product-compliance
Lightning Source LLC
LaVergne TN
LVHW041641070526
838199LV00053B/3502